Mystery Valentine

Adaptation of the animated series: Anne Paradis
Illustrations: Eric Sévigny, based on the animated series

Caillou was still half asleep when Mommy came into his room.
"Happy Valentine's Day, Caillou!"
Now Caillou was wide awake. He had just remembered that his friend Leo had invited him to a party.
"I'm going to make valentines for all my friends," Caillou said.

"That's a great idea," Mommy said. "Valentine's Day is a time to show people how much you care about them." Mommy chose some clothes for Caillou. "This sweater will be perfect," she said. "Red is the colour of love." Caillou could hardly wait to start working on his valentine cards.

Mommy helped Caillou cut out the cards. "Who are you going to give this heart to?" she asked.

"This one is for Clementine. I'm going to stick stars all over it. Where's the glue?" Daddy and Rosie brought the glue to Caillou and left right away. They were laughing. Caillou wondered what was so funny.

Caillou was proud of his valentine cards. He had made special decorations for every one of his friends.

"They're beautiful!" Mommy said. "Your friends will love them."

Caillou was in a hurry to go to the party.

"Don't forget your cards," Daddy said. "I put them in a bag for you."

When Caillou got to Leo's house, all he could think about was giving out his cards.
"Have you started?" he asked.
"No, we were waiting for you," Leo said.
Leo's mommy asked the children, "Are you ready for your valentines?"
"Yeeeeesssss!" all the children shouted at once.

Caillou gave out his first card.
"I made this one for you, Clementine.
Happy Valentine's Day!"
Clementine looked at the card and
beamed. "It's really pretty with all
these stars. Thank you, Caillou."
Then Clementine gave Caillou
a card.
"This is you and me," she said,
and she showed Caillou two
hearts holding hands.

The children handed out their cards and had
heart-shaped cookies for snacks.
"Have you given out all your cards?"
Clementine asked.
Caillou shook his bag, and out fell
a card he hadn't seen before.
"This card isn't mine."
Caillou gave it to Leo's mommy.

Leo's mommy opened the card.
"It's for you, Caillou. Your name is written inside."
Caillou wondered who could have made this card
for him. All of his friends had already given him one.
Leo's mommy said, "It seems to be a mystery card,
Caillou."

Caillou's mommy came to pick him up after the party.
He couldn't wait to show her his mystery card.
"Don't you know who it's from?" asked Mommy.
Caillou shook his head.
"I guess we'll have to investigate!" Mommy said.
Caillou left the party with some heart-shaped cookies
and his valentines.

When Caillou got home, he asked Daddy, "Did you give me this card?"

"No," Daddy said. "Look, there's a cat's paw print on it!"

"It's a valentine from Gilbert!" Caillou exclaimed.

"Hm, I don't think Gilbert would be able to make a card," Daddy said, and he laughed.

Caillou was mystified.

Daddy asked him, "Have you thought of everybody?"

"Hm, there's you, Mommy, Gilbert . . . and Rosie!"

Caillou ran to find his little sister.

"Thank you for this fantastic surprise," he said.

Caillou was very happy. He pulled a big heart-shaped cookie out of his bag and gave it to Rosie.

"Happy Valentine's Day, Rosie!"

Text: adaptation by Anne Paradis of the animated series CAILLOU,
produced by DHX Media Inc.
All rights reserved.
Original story written by Sarah Musgrave and Jason Bogdaneris
Original Episode #170: Mystery Valentine
Illustrations: Eric Sévigny, based on the animated series CAILLOU

The PBS KIDS logo is a registered mark of PBS and is used with permission.

We acknowledge the financial support of the Government of Canada through
the Canada Book Fund for our publishing activities.

■✦■ Canadian   Patrimoine
      Heritage   canadien

We acknowledge the support of the Ministry of Culture and Communications
of Quebec and SODEC for the publication and promotion of this book.

SODEC ■■
  Québec ■■

Bibliothèque et Archives nationales du Québec and Library and Archives
Canada cataloguing in publication

Paradis, Anne, 1972-
[Caillou: mystère à la Saint-Valentin. English]
Caillou: mystery valentine
(Clubhouse)
Translation of: Cailou: mystère à la Saint-Valentin
For children aged 3 and up.

ISBN 978-2-89718-181-9

1. Valentine's Day - Juvenile literature. I. Sévigny, Éric. II. Title. III. Title:
Caillou: mystère à la Saint-Valentin. English. IV. Series: Clubhouse.

GT4925.P3713 2015   j394.2618   C2014-941246-0

Printed in Canada
10 9 8 7 6 5 4 3 2 1 CHO1925 OCT2014